Th

Grandma's Attic

by Judith Benson
illustrated by Shane Hill

A Hodgepog Book

All the characters in this story are fictitious.

Hodgepog Books and The Books Collective acknowledge the ongoing
support of the Canada Council for the Arts for our publishing
program. We also acknowledge the support of the City of Edmonton
and the Edmonton Arts Council.

Editor for the press: Glen Huser.
Managing Editor: Mary Woodbury
Cover illustration and inside illustrations by Shane Hill.
Cover design by Chao Yu. Inside design and page set-up by Ike at the
Wooden Door, in Palatino.

A Hodgepog Book for kids.

Originally published in Canada by Hodgepog Books, an imprint of
The Books Collective, 214-21, 10405 Jasper Avenue, Edmonton,
Alberta, Canada T5J 3S2.

Canadian Cataloguing in Publication Data

Benson, Judith, 1942-
  The noise in Grandma's attic

ISBN 1-895836-55-7

  I. Hill, Shane, 1972- II. Title.
PS8553.E5615N64 1998   jC813'.54   C98-910751-5
PZ7.B44724No 1998

DEDICATION

For all the keen listeners in Mrs. Kimberley's and Miss Epp's 1997-98 classes at Wildwood School

ACKNOWLEDGEMENTS

Thanks to Marion Kimberley who devoted class time to workshop this story with me and to Hodgepog Press for offering me the opportunity to share it with others.

TABLE OF CONTENTS

CHAPTER 1

At Grandma's House

Every Sunday Carla and her dad went in the car to Grandma's house in Prince Albert. Carla's brother Drew came, too.

When they got there, Grandma gave everyone a hug and then she gave them a yummy chicken dinner. She gave them mashed potatoes, red tomatoes and yellow beans. Then she gave them blueberry muffins.

"Yummy yum yum. Yummy yum yum," said Carla. She rubbed her chubby tummy.

"Say with me," said Drew, who liked to say everything Carla said.

Carla rubbed her tummy. Drew rubbed his tummy.

They said, "Yummy yum yum. Yummy yum yum."

"Thank you, Grandma," said Dad.

"Thank you, Grandma," said Carla. Carla was seven and knew about good manners.

"Tank you, Gamma," said Drew. Drew was three and didn't always get his words just right.

Dad said, "We will wash the dishes while you rest, Grandma."

Grandma said, "Okay," and went upstairs.

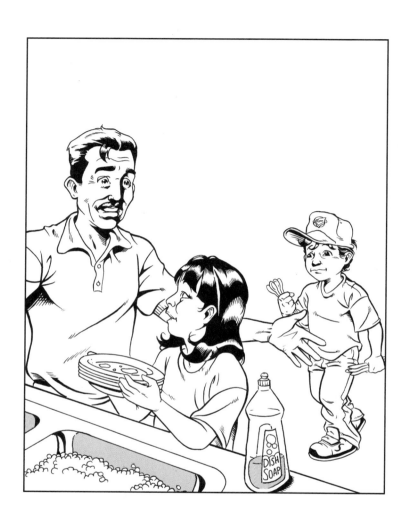

4

CHAPTER 2

The Tappity Tap Noise

Dad ran the hot water.

Drew said, "Up up up, Daddy."

Drew pulled on one of Dad's
ears. His ears stuck out from his
head and Drew liked to pull them.

"Ouch!" Dad said and laughed.

Drew put in the dish soap. "Bubbles, bubbles, pop pop pop," he said.

Dad took the glasses to the sink. Carla took the plates and forks to the sink. Drew took the spoons.

They all sang the *Magic Penny* song. Then Carla heard a funny noise.

Tappity tap. Tappity tap. Tappity tappity. Tap tap tap.

"What is that noise?" asked Carla.

"What noise?" asked Dad.

Carla said, "It went tappity tap. Tappity tap. Tappity tappity. Tap tap tap."

"I say it," said Drew.

Carla said the noise with Drew.

"Tappity tap. Tappity tap. Tappity tappity. Tap tap tap."

"I'm scared," said Carla.

"Don't be scared," Dad said. "The woodpecker goes tappity tap on the old elm tree. Let's look outside."

Carla and Drew ran out the back door. The door went crash. They ran to one side of the house.

"No birds here," said Carla.

"No birdies," said Drew.

They ran to the other side of the house.

"No birds here," said Carla.

"No birdies," said Drew.

Dad ran to the front of the house. "No woodpeckers here," he said. "Let's go inside and dry the dishes.

CHAPTER 3

The Slide Slide Slide Noise

Carla dried the plates and forks. Dad dried the glasses. Drew dried the spoons.

Then Carla and Drew made the

dish towels go around and around. They ran around the kitchen and up and down the hall. "They will dry fast this way," said Carla.

"Fast fast!" said Drew.

"Hush, you two," said Dad. "Grandma is resting."

"Oh, I forgot," said Carla. Then she heard a funny noise.

"What is that noise?" asked Carla.

"What noise?" asked Dad.

Carla said, "It went slide slide slide. Slide slide slide."

"I say it," said Drew.

Carla said the noise with Drew. "Slide slide slide. Slide slide slide."

"I'm scared," said Carla.

"Don't be scared," Dad said. "A tree branch makes a slide slide slide noise when it hits the side of the house. Let's look outside."

Carla and Drew ran out the back door. They ran to one side of the house.

"No branches here," said Carla.

"No banches," said Drew.

They ran to the other side of the house.

14

"No branches here," said Carla.

"No banches," said Drew.

Dad ran to the front of the house. "No branches here," he said. "Let's go inside and put the dishes away."

CHAPTER 4

The Thumpity Thump Noise

Carla put the forks away. Dad put the plates and glasses away. Drew put the spoons away.

"Hurray!" said Carla. "We are all

done!" She jumped up and down.
"All done! All done!" Drew said.
He jumped up and down, too.
"Hush, you two," said Dad.
"Grandma is resting."
"Forgot," said Drew.

Then they heard a funny noise.

Thumpity thump. Thumpity thump. Thumpity thumpity. Thump thump thump.

"What is that noise?" Carla asked.

"I heard a noise, too," said Dad. "It went thumpity thump. Thumpity thump. Thumpity thumpity. Thump thump thump."

"I say it," said Drew.

They all said it together. "Thumpity thump. Thumpity thump. Thumpity thumpity. Thump thump thump."

"It's not outside the house," said Carla.

"No. It's inside the house," said Dad.

"Inside out," said Drew.

They all laughed. But then Carla said, "I'm scared."

Dad said, "Don't be scared. Drew and I are with you. Let's go look."

20

CHAPTER 5

Where is the Noise?

Dad looked in the living room. Carla and Drew looked in the bathroom.

"No tappity tap," said Drew.

"Let's look upstairs," said Carla.

"Up up up," said Drew.

"Hush," said Dad. "Grandma is

resting." He put his finger over his lips. Carla and Drew did, too.

They all said, "Hush hush hush. Hush hush hush."

Dad looked in the extra bedroom. He turned around and shook his head. Carla and Drew looked in the bathroom.

"No slide slide," said Drew. "Gotta go, Daddy."

Dad took Drew into the bathroom. When they came out Dad said, "Let's peek into Grandma's room."

They all peeked in.

"No Grandma," said Dad.

"Where is Grandma?" Carla asked.

Drew walked into the bedroom. He looked under the bed. He looked under the dresser. He looked in the closet. "No Gamma," he said. "Where's Gamma?"

CHAPTER 6

The Noise in Grandma's Attic

Tap tap tap.
"I hear a noise," said Dad.
Slide slide slide.
"I hear a noise, too," said Carla.

Thump thump thump.

"Me, too," said Drew.

"Let's look up in the attic," said Dad.

"What's the attic?" asked Carla.

"It's a place where no one lives. It is a place to store things."

"Is it scary?" asked Carla.

"It's scary if you are alone," said Dad. "We are not alone. We are together."

"Is it dark?" asked Carla.

"It may be dark," said Dad. "I will get a flashlight from Grandma's room. Wait here for me."

Dad came back and handed the flashlight to Carla. "Let's go," he said.

"Go," said Drew.

Carla turned on the flashlight and followed Dad up the attic stairs. Drew followed Carla.

Up up up they went. The noise went tappity tap. Tappity tap.

Tappity tappity. Tap tap tap. Slide slide slide. Slide slide slide. Thumpity thump. Thumpity thump. Thumpity thumpity. Thump thump thump.

"I'm scared," said Carla.

"Take my hand," said Dad.

"Scary," said Drew. He took Carla's hand.

They went up some more. The noise was very loud.

"Let's peek in the attic door," said Dad as he opened it slowly.

They all peeked in. They saw Grandma. She wore a pink

29

sweatsuit and black and white dancing shoes. She held her arms out to the sides. She did not see them.

Her feet went tappity tap. She did a step to one side. Her feet went slide slide slide. She jumped up. She came down thumpity thump. Then she saw them peeking at her.

"Oh! You scared me!" she said.

"You scared us, Grandma!" said Dad.

Carla looked at Grandma. "We heard the noise, Grandma. We

came to find the noise."

"What noise?" asked Grandma.

Drew said, "Tappity tap."

Carla said, "Slide slide slide."

Dad said, "And thumpity thump."

"Oh," said Grandma. "I was dancing. I'm taking dancing lessons. I didn't mean to scare you. Did I make lots of noise?"

"Yes, Grandma," said Drew.

"Grandma," said Carla. "Drew said your name right!"

"Good for you, Drew!" Grandma smiled with her mouth and her

eyes. She patted Drew's head.

Dad said, "Well, what do you all want to do now?"

"Grandma dance," Drew said. "Drew dance. Carla dance. Daddy dance, too."

Carla laughed. "What a fun idea!" So they took each other's hands and danced in a line. Tappity tap. Tappity tap. Tappity tappity. Tap tap tap. Slide slide slide. Slide slide slide. Thumpity thump. Thumpity thump. Thumpity thumpity. Thump thump thump.

"Now I am tired," said Grandma.
"I am tired, too," said Dad.
"You tired, Carla?" Drew asked.
"A little," she said.
"Drew, too," said Drew.
Then they all went downstairs
to rest.

The End

About the Author

Judith Benson was born in Joliet, Illinois, and studied at University of Michigan before starting her teaching career in Manchester, England. Since 1974 she has lived and taught in Canada, and has become a Canadian citizen. She now lives in Saskatoon where she writes, works for the preservation of American elms, restoration of wildlife habitat and promotes environmental education. She and her husband Geoff enjoy holidays with their two grown children and granddaughters.

About the Artist

Shane Hill's love of cartooning took him all the way to New Jersey, where he attended the Joe Kubert School of Cartoon and Graphic Art. After graduation, Shane moved back home to Edmonton, Alberta, where he works for a local design firm. Shane's artwork is in a number of private collections in western Canada. His dream is someday to become a professional comic book artist. *The Noise in Grandma's Attic* is his third book project.

If you liked this book...
you might enjoy these other Hodgepog books:

Read them yourself in grades 4-5, or read them to younger kids!

A Gift for Johnny Know-It-All
by Mary Woodbury, illustrated by Barbara Hartmann
ISBN 1-895836-27-1   Price: $5.95

A Real Farm Girl
by Susan Ioannou, illustrated by James Rozak
ISBN 1-895836-52-2   Price: $6.95

Arly and Spike
by Luanne Armstrong, illustrated by Chao Yu
ISBN 1-895836-37-9   Price: $4.95

Mill Creek Kids
by Colleen Heffernan, illustrated by Sonja Zacharias
ISBN 1-895836-40-9   Price: $5.95

A Friend for Mr. Granville
by Gillian Richardson, illustrated by Claudette MacLean
ISBN 1-895836-38-7   Price: $5.95

Ben and the Carrot Predicament
by Mar'ce Merrell, illustrated by Barbara Hartmann
ISBN 1-895836-54-9   Price: $5.95

Getting Rid of Mr. Ribitus
by Alison Lohans, illustrated by Barbara Hartmann
ISBN 1-895836-53-0   Price: $5.95

and for readers in grades 1-2, or to read to pre-schoolers:

Summer With Sebastian
by Gwen Molnar, illustrated by Kendra McCleskey
ISBN 1-895836-39-5   Price: $4.95

Teachers Guides Available. Write or fax:
Hodgepog Books, 214-21 10405 Jasper Avenue, Edmonton, Alberta,
Canada T5J 3S2, ph. (403) 448 0590 fax (403) 448 0640